Meet the Kreeps

Titles in the series

Meet the Kreeps

Kiki Thorpe

SCHOLASTIC

Scholastic Children's Books
An imprint of Scholastic Ltd
Euston House, 24 Eversholt Street
London, NW1 1DB, UK
Registered office: Westfield Road, Southam, Warwickshire, CV47 0RA
SCHOLASTIC and associated logos are trademarks and/or registered
trademarks of Scholastic Inc.

First published in the US in 2008 by Scholastic Inc.
This edition published in the UK by Scholastic Ltd, 2009

Text copyright © Kiki Thorpe, 2008
The right of Kiki Thorpe to be identified as the author of this work has
been asserted by her.

ISBN 978 1407 11009 7

Printed in the UK by CPI Bookmarque, Croydon
Papers used by Scholastic Children's Books are made
from wood grown in sustainable forests.

1 3 5 7 9 10 8 6 4 2

www.scholastic.co.uk/zone

For Greg

❧ Chapter 1 ❧

Polly Winkler was not exactly nosy, but she did have a lot of curiosity. And right now it was blazing.

"*Weird!*" she exclaimed. She sat straight up and stared out her living room window. Across the street, two men were unloading something from the back of a removal van. It had a long snout, an even longer tail, and looked an awful lot like a crocodile.

"What's weird?" asked her friend Mike, looking up from his homework.

"I just saw a crocodile," Polly told him.

"A *crocodile*? Where?" asked Mike.

"There." Polly shook her long sandy fringe

out of her eyes and blinked. The crocodile was gone.

"I mean, I thought I saw. . ." Polly got up and went over to the window. Two removal men were carrying a sofa up the walkway of the house across the street. There was no sign of a giant reptile.

"Never mind," she told Mike.

Mike shrugged and went back to his homework.

Polly watched the removal men struggle up the walkway. *There is something funny about that sofa*, she thought. For one thing, the back was shaped like pointy wings. And the sofa's gold feet looked like—

"Claws," Polly said with a little shiver.

"Huh?" said Mike.

"I just saw a sofa shaped like a bat!" Polly told him.

"What are you talking about?" Mike asked.

"Across the street! Look!" Polly pointed out the window.

"I don't see anything," Mike said.

"You just missed it! They must have taken it into the house," Polly said. "It looked like it belonged in one of those old black-and-white horror films!" *Not in our extremely normal neighbourhood,* she added to herself.

Then again, the house across the street didn't really look like it belonged in her neighbourhood, either. It was a big, old wooden heap, with two pointy towers like witches' hats. The shutters sagged on their hinges, and ivy crawled up the walls. Next to the neat little houses on Pleasant Street, the mansion reminded Polly of a big grey vulture roosting in a hen-house.

"I can't believe someone is moving into that old dump," she said.

3

"What *I* can't believe is that we have to write three pages without using the Internet," Mike complained, throwing down his pencil.

"I know," Polly said. She went over to the sofa and sat back down. "I never thought year five would be so hard."

"I'm going to have my mum help me with my project," Mike said. "She's been to Germany, so I figure she can tell me all about it. Which country are you doing?"

"Moldova," Polly told him.

Mike wrinkled his nose. "Moldova?"

"What's wrong with Moldova?" Polly asked.

"Er, nothing," Mike said. "But why'd you pick that?"

"It looked small on the map," Polly said with a shrug. "So I thought it would be easy. Anyway, I'm not too worried. We have two whole weeks before it's due."

"Moldova," Mike mumbled, shaking his head. "You're funny, Polly."

But Polly didn't hear him. She was staring out the window again. The two removal men were unloading a jumbo-sized box from the back of the van. As they swung it around, Polly caught a glimpse of the writing on the side. KITCHEN: SWORDS AND SKEWERS, it read.

"Mike!" she squeaked, jumping to her feet. "Do you see that? Totally freaky!"

Mike got up and ambled over to the window. "What's so freaky about a TV?" he asked.

Polly looked again. Now she could see that it was like the kind of box that a TV came in.

"You missed it!" she cried. "It's not a TV. The box said SWORDS in big letters on the side. I saw it!"

Mike grinned and folded his arms. "Just

5

like the crocodile and the bat-shaped sofa, right? Are you sure you didn't imagine it?"

"I saw it! I swear!" Polly insisted. "Anyway, if you want proof that there's something weird going on over there, just take a look at *her*."

Across the street, a tall, pale woman was paying the removal men. Although the day was warm, she wore a dark, long-sleeved dress, and boots with pointy toes. Her long black hair hung down to her waist. Earrings shaped like beetles dangled from her earlobes.

"Whoa!" Mike's eyes widened. "She looks like she's ready to go trick-or-treating!"

"Told you." Polly couldn't resist a smirk.

As the removal van pulled away, Polly suddenly noticed three kids out in front of the old mansion: a teenage boy dressed all in black, a younger boy with hair that stood up like porcupine quills, and a little girl with two black pigtails. The girl's eyes were so big and round that even from across the street Polly could tell they were green.

"Those must be her kids," Mike said.

"They look just like her – weird," Polly said. Then she did a double take. "Wait! Is that spiky-haired kid wearing rubber gloves? That's *beyond* weird."

"Where do you think they're from?" said Mike.

"Transylvania," Polly joked. She and Mike laughed.

Just then the Winklers' living room clock chimed. "Uh-oh. I gotta go!" Mike said, hopping up. "I told my mum I'd be home early because of the supper at school." Polly and Mike's class was holding an international food evening, as part of their Geography project on different countries.

"What are you bringing?" Polly asked.

"Mum's making German chocolate cake," said Mike. "What about you?"

"I'm not sure yet," Polly told him. "I couldn't find any recipes from Moldova. But my dad said he'd whip something up when he gets home from work."

Mike picked up his backpack and headed for the door. "See you later."

"See you," said Polly. She waved as Mike headed out the door, then turned back to the window.

But when she looked across the street again, the strange family had vanished.

⚜ Chapter 2 ⚜

O K, buckaroos! We're almost ready to roll!" Polly's dad called.

Polly looked up from the book she was reading and sighed. Her dad always thought he was so funny. She could smell something spicy cooking. *Uh-oh,* she thought, *that smells like Dad's chilli!*

She followed her nose to the kitchen. Sure enough, her dad was standing at the cooker, stirring something in a pot.

"Grab a taste of this boss grub," he told Polly. That was his funny cowboy talk for "good food". Dr Winkler was a dentist who had never set foot in the Wild West, but he claimed his chilli was an old cowboy recipe. Whenever he made it, he served it up in bowls with spoons, like the family were cowboys sitting around a campfire.

The back door opened, and Polly's older sister, Joy, bounced into the kitchen. As usual, she was wearing her cheerleading uniform and a big smile. "Hey, Polly. Hey, Dad. What's cooking?" she asked.

"Chocolate chilli," Polly told her. "For the international supper at school tonight."

"Uh-oh," said Joy. Her smile faded.

"You'll love it," their dad assured them. "It's just like they make in Mexico! Only I couldn't find Mexican chocolate. So I used Mars bars. Here, try some." He held out a spoon.

Joy backed away. "No, thanks. I'm, er, not hungry right now. But I'll bet Petey will try it!" she said brightly, as their younger brother walked in.

"Have a taste of chilli, Petey," said Dr Winkler.

Petey took a tiny bite. *"Gaack!"* he choked.

"Too spicy?" asked their dad.

Petey took off his glasses and wiped his eyes. "Y-u-c-k," he said.

"I have an idea! Let's bring chips and guacamole to the school supper, too," Joy suggested. She hurried over to the cupboard and refrigerator to get them out.

"We shouldn't bring chilli *or* chips *or* guacamole," Polly said. "My project is on Moldova, not Mexico."

"Moldova?" Dr Winkler scratched his head. "I was sure you said *Mexico*. Well, don't worry. We can pick some up at the shop on our way there. Tasty stuff, that Moldova. A little like Gorgonzola, isn't it?"

Polly sighed. "It's a country, Dad. Not a cheese."

"Oh, right," he said. "Speaking of cheese, do you know what you call a cheese that isn't yours?"

"What?" asked Polly.

"Nacho cheese!"

"D-a-a-ad!" Polly rolled her eyes. But she couldn't help giggling. Her dad's cooking stank, but his jokes always made her laugh.

"Nacho!" Petey piped up. "That's n-a-c-h-o." Petey was eight and his dream was to win the school spelling competition. He'd been practising for months.

"'Nacho' is easy. Try 'guacamole'," said Polly, who liked to keep him on his toes.

Petey pushed his glasses up on his nose. "G-u-a-c-a-m-o-l-e," he said.

"Great job, cowboy," said Dr Winkler. "You're going to blow them away at the spelling competition—"

Dr Winkler's mobile phone rang,

interrupting him. He checked the caller ID. "I'd better take this. It's the root canal I did this afternoon," he said. He headed into the living room. "Hello, Mrs Spitz," they heard him say. "How are you feeling?"

"Mrrrrrmlllllfffg?" Petey asked.

"Huh?" Polly glanced over at her brother. His mouth was stuffed so full of tortilla chips that he looked like a chipmunk.

"I said, when are we leaving for the school supper?" Petey asked, spattering her with crumbs.

"Petey! That's disgusting." Polly wiped herself with her napkin. "When are you going to learn to eat like a human being?" she demanded.

Petey shrugged. "In year five?" He wiped his mouth on the back of his hand.

"You'll be in a zoo before you *get* to year five," Polly told him. "Use a napkin at least!"

Petey stuck his finger in his nose and probed. Then he wiped it on a napkin.

"Petey!" Polly and Joy exclaimed in unison.

"What?" he said. "I used a napkin!"

"Dad!" Polly looked to her father, who had just returned to the kitchen. "Tell Petey!"

"Tell him what, honey?" Her father looked at her blankly.

"He—" Polly began.

Bleeeeeeeeeeeeeeeeeeeeeeep! The piercing shriek of the smoke alarm cut her off. Huge clouds of smoke were billowing from the pot on the stove.

"The chilli!" Dr Winkler cried.

He rushed to the stove. Joy and Polly ran to open the kitchen windows. Petey grabbed a broom and began to whack at the alarm.

Another typical night at the Winkler house, Polly thought.

Dr Winkler waved a dishcloth over the smoking pot. "I think it's OK," he said. "It will just have a nice – er, smoky flavour."

Polly turned to Joy. "Maybe we'd better bring those chips and guacamole after all," she whispered.

The Endsville Primary School canteen was crowded with families who had come for the international food evening. As soon as she walked in, Polly spotted Mike standing near the dessert table.

"Hey, Polly," Mike said as she came over. He frowned and sniffed the air. "Do you smell smoke?"

"It's probably me," Polly told him. "Dad burned the food again. Speaking of which, stay away from the chilli."

"Who needs chilli when you can have

pudding for dinner?" Mike pointed to his paper plate, which was piled with cake and cookies. "Try some German chocolate cake," he said. "That's the one my mum made."

"Yum," said Polly, serving herself a slice. "Maybe this project isn't so bad after all."

She was about to dig into a plate of brownies when Mike tugged her arm. "Look out," he said. "Here comes Denise."

A girl with curly brown hair walked over to them. She was carrying a tray of fancy-looking cookies.

"These are French lace cookies," she announced as she set the tray down. "My mother made them. She's been to Paris three times, you know. She knows everything about France. That's why I'm sure my project will be the best."

Mike looked at Polly and rolled his eyes.

Denise picked up a French lace cookie.

She held her pinkie out as she took a tiny nibble. "*Très bon.* That means 'very good' in French. What did you bring to the international supper?" she asked Polly and Mike.

"German chocolate cake," Mike told her. "Since my country is Germany."

"We brought – er. . ." Polly hesitated. She wasn't sure she wanted the whole school to know about her dad's chilli disaster.

At that moment, Dr Winkler walked over, carrying the pot of chilli. "Hey, buckaroos, do you think chocolate chilli is a main course or a dessert?" he asked.

"Chocolate *chilli*?" Denise stuck out her tongue. "Gross!"

"Don't knock it till you try it. It's a special recipe from Moldova," Dr Winkler said, giving Polly a wink. "Let's say it's a dessert." He set the pot down and headed off to talk to some other parents.

Denise turned to Polly, her eyes wide. "Your dad brought *mouldy* chocolate chilli? That's grosser than gross!"

"Not mouldy," Polly told her. "Moldova. It's the country I'm doing my project on."

"You're weird, Polly," Denise said. Then she turned and flounced away.

"She's so full of herself," Mike grumbled.

"Yeah," Polly agreed.

"Come on, let's find a place to sit," Mike said.

"I'm going to get something to drink," Polly told him. "I'll be there in a minute."

As Mike headed off, Polly wandered over to the table that had fizzy drinks and juice. She was just pouring herself a cup of apple juice, when she heard someone say, "Polly Winkler is so weird."

Polly froze, still holding her cup of juice. It was a girl's voice talking.

"Did you know her dad brought mouldy

18

chocolate chilli to the school supper?" the girl went on. "Have you ever heard of anything more disgusting?"

Denise! Polly thought. But where was she?

Polly peeked around a corner of the canteen. Denise was sitting on the other side of the wall, talking to another girl in their class. Where Polly was standing, they couldn't see her.

"And have you ever seen her little brother eat?" Denise went on. "He acts like a pig!"

Polly felt her cheeks grow hot. *Petey!* she thought furiously. *I told him to use a napkin!*

"But they really can't help it," Denise said. "It's because they don't have a mum."

Polly swallowed hard. It was true that she didn't have a mum. Her mother had died when Polly was very young, so long ago that Polly barely remembered her.

19

Polly didn't want to hear any more. With a lump in her throat, she crept away.

"Hey, what took you so long?" Mike asked as she walked up to the table where he was sitting. "I almost ate your cake."

"You can have it. I'm not hungry any more," Polly said. She pushed her plate towards him.

Polly watched as Mike grabbed his fork and dug in. "Hey, Mike, do you think I'm weird?" she asked.

"Sure," Mike said between bites. "I think you're a total lunatic for not wanting this cake."

"But do you think my family's weird?" Polly asked.

Mike shrugged. "I don't know. Can I have a sip of your juice?"

Polly sighed and handed him her cup. She couldn't stop thinking about what Denise had said. Maybe it was true that the

Winklers were weird. After all, they didn't have a mum. And mums were important.

Mums made chocolate cake, not chocolate chilli.

Mums helped you with your homework.

Mums knew all about table manners.

Mums didn't set off the smoke alarm every time they cooked.

What the Winklers need is a mum, Polly decided. *And I'm going to find her.*

❖ Chapter 3 ❖

The next day after school, Polly and Mike stood on the Winklers' front porch. Polly was wearing binoculars around her neck. A notebook was tucked into her back pocket.

"Now, tell me what we're doing again?" Mike asked.

"We're launching Mission Mum," Polly said.

"Mission Mum?" Mike asked, scratching his head.

Polly nodded. "My family needs a mum. And we're going to find one. Starting today."

"How are we going to do that?" Mike wondered.

"Don't worry. I've got it all figured out." Polly whipped her notebook out of her back pocket and read, "*Step One: we find a good mum. Step Two: she meets my dad. Step Three: they fall in love and get married.*" She looked at Mike and grinned. "Easy!"

"You really think that'll work?" Mike asked.

"It *has* to work," Polly said. "My dad burns dinner almost every night. My brother eats like a pig. And my sister's too busy cheerleading to do anything else. We really need a mum."

"It sounds to me like you need a maid," said Mike.

Polly put her hands on her hips. "Are you going to help me or what?" she asked.

Mike shrugged. "Sure. How do we start?"

"Well," Polly said, looking around, "do you see any good mums?"

Mike pointed down the street. "What about her?"

Polly lifted her binoculars. At the end of the street, an old woman was walking her little dog. They were inching along at a snail's pace.

"That's Miss Crumper," Polly said. "She's too old to be our mum."

"OK. Then how about her?" Mike suggested. He pointed to a young woman who was riding past on her bike, her ponytail whipping in the wind.

"Uh-uh," Polly said. "That's Jennifer Armstrong. She just left college last year. Way too young to be our mum."

"Jeez, you're picky," Mike said. "This could take all day." He sat down on Polly's front steps. Polly sat down next to him.

Just then, a flash of pink across the

street caught her eye. It was Miss Tulip, who lived in the house next to the old mansion. She was out working in her front garden.

Polly watched her kneel down and carefully pull out the weeds around a rosebush. *Hmm*, Polly thought. She took a closer look at Miss Tulip's house. The garden was neatly trimmed, and pretty pink curtains hung in the windows.

"Miss Tulip could be our mum!" she said.

Mike followed her gaze. "Her? She's awfully . . . pink."

Polly nodded. "I've never seen her wear anything but pink. Pink jeans, pink T-shirts, pink coats – she even has pink trainers. Pink is a good colour for a mum, don't you think?"

"My mum hates pink," Mike said.

Polly shrugged. She took her notebook out of her pocket and wrote: *Miss Tulip?*

Polly tapped her pencil on her lips. "I wonder if she can cook," she said.

"What if her whole kitchen is pink?" Mike said.

Polly laughed. She imagined Miss Tulip cooking on a pink hob next to a big pink refrigerator. "And all the food is pink, too!" she said. "Like pink ham."

"Pink cupcakes," Mike added.

"Pink smoothies!"

"Pink ice cream!"

"Pink strawberry angel-food cake!" Just the thought made Polly's mouth water. Miss Tulip was starting to seem like the perfect mum!

Creeeeeeeeeeeeeeeeeeeeeeeeeeeeeeeeeeeak.

A noise like a coffin opening made Polly and Mike jump. The front door of the old mansion slowly opened. Out stepped Polly's new neighbour. She was still wearing her long black dress, but today she'd added elbow-length gloves and a big, floppy black hat.

"She looks like a witch!" Polly whispered to Mike.

"What's that she's carrying?" Mike wondered. "It looks like some kind of flower."

Polly raised her binoculars. "A flower crossed with a lizard is more like it. I'm pretty sure that thing has teeth!"

They watched as the woman went over to the empty flower bed and started to dig.

As if she felt their eyes on her, the woman suddenly turned. She fixed them with a green-eyed stare.

Polly and Mike both gasped.

But then the woman smiled. It was a perfectly ordinary, friendly smile. "Hello there!" she called.

"Er . . . hi," Polly called back.

"Lovely day, isn't it?" the woman said.

Polly blinked and looked up at the sky. It was full of dark clouds. "Is she joking?" she whispered to Mike. He shrugged.

The woman continued to smile pleasantly, as if she was waiting for them to agree.

"Uh, sure," Polly said. She stood up and brushed off the seat of her trousers. She had more important things to do than talk to the nutty new neighbour.

But as she was about to leave, Mike suddenly called to the woman, "What are you planting?"

"Venus flytraps," the woman said. "Come take a look, if you like."

"Cool!" Mike hopped to his feet.

"What are you doing?" Polly whispered to him. "You can't go over there!"

"Why not?" Mike asked.

"Because she's *weird*!" Polly said.

"She seems nice," Mike said. "Besides, I want to see a Venus flytrap."

As Mike crossed the street, Polly frowned and folded her arms. Mike was supposed to be helping her, not talking to the weirdo neighbours! But her curiosity got the better of her. A moment later, she followed him.

"I didn't know Venus flytraps got this big!" Mike said as he examined the plants.

"So, they mostly eat flies, right?" Polly asked nervously. Was it her imagination, or were the plants looking at her in a hungry sort of way?

"That's right," said the woman. "But they won't say no to a good steak. I'm Veronica Kreep, by the way. But you can call me Veronica."

"I'm Mike," said Mike. "And this is Polly. She lives across the street." Polly scowled at him.

But Veronica looked delighted. "My

children will be so excited to meet you," she said. "They don't know anyone in the neighbourhood yet."

Just then, the door of the house opened again. The teenage boy Polly had seen the day before flew down the front steps on his skateboard. He whipped past Polly and Mike without a second glance.

"Stop right there," Veronica commanded.

The boy kicked his skateboard to a stop. With a sigh, he skulked back to his mother. He wore a black sweatshirt with the hood pulled over his head. Polly noticed his face was as pale as a vampire's.

"Vincent, meet Polly and Mike. Vincent is my oldest son," Veronica told them.

"Hello," Vincent mumbled from beneath his hood.

"He doesn't *seem* excited to meet us," Polly whispered to Mike.

"Did you feed the snakes?" Veronica asked Vincent.

"Yes," he said.

"Did you put on enough sunscreen?" Veronica asked.

Vincent rolled his eyes. "Yes, Mother."

"All right, you can go." Before the words were even out of Veronica's mouth, Vincent was speeding away.

"Don't mind him," Veronica said to Polly and Mike. "He's just getting used to being here. Endsville is so different from the last town we lived in." She turned to shout after Vincent, "Be back before dawn! And stay out of the cemetery this time!"

Dawn? Cemetery?! Polly thought. *Who are these people?*

Veronica smiled. "We must seem pretty different to you. We're probably the only Witch –"

Polly's eyes widened.

"– itans you've met," Veronica finished.

"Wichitans?" asked Polly and Mike in unison.

"From Wichita, Kansas," Veronica explained. "Though we have family all over the world."

Everything about the Kreeps is as weird as their last name, Polly thought. And she'd had enough weirdness for now. "It was nice to meet you," she told Veronica. "But we have to go. We have loads of, um, homework to do."

Mike looked at her. "No we—"

Before he could finish, Polly grabbed his arm and dragged him away.

"Be sure to come back!" Veronica called after them. "I know Damon and Esmerelda will be dying to meet you."

Not if I can help it, Polly thought.

❋ Chapter 4 ❋

Hideous'," Polly told Petey.

"H-i-d-e-o-u-s," he replied.

"Right," said Polly. "How about 'abominable'."

Petey spelled that correctly, too.

Polly looked down the list of spelling words. "Petey, you already know these," she said. "I don't see why we have to go through them again."

"You promised!" Petey whined. "We made a deal!"

Polly had finally struck a bargain with her brother. She agreed to drill him on spelling words every night, so long as he followed a few simple rules: use a knife and fork. Don't talk with your mouth full. And "use a tissue instead of your finger," she reminded him as he reached for his nose.

Petey plucked a tissue from the box and blew.

"Petey, why do you want to win this spelling competition so badly?" Polly asked him.

"I don't know. I just do," said Petey.

The smell of tomato sauce wafted from the Winklers' kitchen. *Spaghetti*, Polly thought with a shudder. She hoped her dad wasn't trying another "experiment".

It's time to get on with Mission Mum, Polly thought, glancing out the window. She could see Miss Tulip standing in her front garden, admiring the sunset. The warm light deepened the pink of her dress and made her face look especially rosy.

Now is the perfect time for them to meet! thought Polly. *This could be so romantic!*

"Listen, Petey. We'll finish this later," she said, shoving the word list back at him. "Dad!" she yelled. "Come here! Hurry!"

Dr Winkler rushed out of the kitchen, still wearing his sauce-spattered apron. "What is it?" he asked. "Is someone bleeding?"

"No, Dad. You need to see this beautiful sunset," Polly told him.

Her dad sighed. "Polly," he said, "I really don't have time. . ."

But Polly began pulling him towards the door. "You know what they say. You have to stop and smell the roses now and then."

When they got outside, Polly was relieved to see that Miss Tulip was still standing in her front garden. "Miss Tulip!" she yelled over to her. "Come watch the sunset with us! The view's better from here."

"Polly," her dad whispered, "I really don't think that's a good— Well, hello, Lobelia!" he said as Miss Tulip stepped on to their porch.

"Hello, Wally," she replied.

First names, thought Polly. *Excellent!* She retreated to the far end of the porch to watch them talk.

"So, how is business these days?" Miss Tulip asked her dad.

"Oh, you know. Plenty of toothaches keeping me busy," Dr Winkler said.

Miss Tulip nodded and smiled. But then her eyes fell on the Winklers' front lawn. Instantly, her smile vanished. "What is *that*?" she exclaimed.

Dr Winkler looked where she was pointing. "A dandelion?" he said.

"A dandelion!" Miss Tulip huffed. "And do you know what a dandelion is?"

"Er, pretty?" Dr Winkler guessed.

"It's a weed!" Miss Tulip screeched.

Uh-oh, thought Polly.

Dr Winkler gave Miss Tulip a pained smile. "It's just one small dandelion—"

"Before you know it, that 'one small dandelion' will be blowing its seeds everywhere!" she bellowed. "All it would take is one gust of wind to ruin my whole garden!" Miss Tulip's face was now as pink as her dress. Dr Winkler had started to look like *he* was the one with a toothache.

Meanwhile, the clouds behind the old mansion were changing from red to a brilliant grape-like purple.

"Wow! This sunset just keeps getting better," Polly said loudly, hoping to distract them.

Everyone turned to look at the sky, which suddenly turned from purple to violent green.

"You're right, Polly," said her dad. "This *is* quite a sunset."

"But . . . surely that isn't the sunset," Miss Tulip said. She sounded worried.

She's right, thought Polly. *But what is it?*

The clouds had now formed a dense fog around the Kreeps' house. Suddenly, Polly realized they weren't clouds at all.

"It's smoke!" she exclaimed. The thick, green smoke was billowing from the Kreeps' basement!

"I wonder if I should call the fire brigade," Dr Winkler said.

Just then, Veronica Kreep came strolling out her front door. When she saw them all staring at her, she waved.

"Hello!" she called. "Lovely night, isn't it?"

"Do you know there's green smoke coming out of your house?" Dr Winkler yelled to her.

Veronica looked around. "Oh, dear. You're right," she said.

She calmly walked over and rapped on the basement window. A moment later, Damon's spiky head appeared. He was wearing giant goggles that made him look like an insect. "Darling!" Veronica said. "There's green smoke!"

"Sorry, Mother," Damon said. He disappeared back into the basement.

A second later, the smoke changed. Now it was blue.

Veronica smiled. "Much better! Damon's our scientist," she explained, walking over to the Winklers' front porch. "He's very talented. But he still makes mistakes now and then. After all, he's only ten."

Miss Tulip covered her nose. "That smoke smells terrible," she complained. "It's not poisonous, is it?"

"Hardly at all," Veronica said brightly.

No sooner were the words out of her mouth than a gust of wind came up. It blew the clouds of smoke straight into Miss Tulip's front garden. Her garden disappeared into a blue fog.

When the fog cleared, they saw that all the petals had fallen off Miss Tulip's pink flowers.

Miss Tulip gasped. "My petunias!" she squealed. "My roses! My zinnias!" She went scurrying back to her garden.

"Now, that's too bad. I hope they grow back," Dr Winkler said. But the corners of his moustache twitched. Polly could tell he was trying not to smile. He turned to Veronica and held out his hand. "Wally Winkler," he said.

"Veronica Kreep," she replied, shaking it. "Nice to meet you."

"Polly," her dad said, "you were right. Sometimes you do just need to stop and smell the roses – or what's left of them," he added, with a glance at Miss Tulip's garden.

With a sigh, Polly took out her notebook and crossed Miss Tulip's name off her list.

❧ Chapter 5 ❧

"A ny luck yet?" Mike asked the next afternoon.

Polly shook her head. They had come to the public library to look for books for their projects. But so far, Polly hadn't been able to find a single thing on Moldova. "I'm starting to think this country doesn't even exist!" she told Mike.

"*Shhhhhhh!*" Miss Maus, the librarian, looked up from her desk and held a finger to her lips.

Polly sat down at a table and got out her notebook. *The project can wait for now*, she thought. *Time for phase two of Mission Mum.*

Polly had decided that she needed to get organized. *In order to find a good mum,* she thought, *I have to know what we're looking for.* She shook her fringe out of her eyes, turned to a fresh page in her notebook, and wrote:

Our Perfect Mum:
1. Neat and tidy
2. A good cook
3. Helpful with homework

Polly chewed the end of her pencil, then added:

4. Interested in teeth

Was it important for her new mum to have hobbies? Polly wasn't sure. She leaned over to Mike. "Hey, do you think—"

"*Shhhhhhhhhhh!*" Miss Maus was looking up at her again.

"Sorry!" Polly mouthed.

Miss Maus gave her a little smile. Then she turned back to the stacks of books she was sorting. She worked briskly, placing every book in a tidy pile.

Hmm, Polly thought. She looked at Miss Maus more closely, noting her clean white blouse, her sharply pleated grey skirt and her shiny black shoes.

She's definitely neat, thought Polly. *And she must be helpful with homework. After all, she's a librarian!* Polly wondered if Miss Maus liked to cook, or if she had any interest in teeth.

There was a bigger question, though: how was she going to get her dad and Miss Maus to meet? He hardly ever came to the library.

Just then, she noticed a neatly lettered sign on Miss Maus's desk. It read:

ANNUAL BOOK SALE TO BENEFIT THE LIBRARY! THIS SATURDAY! ALL DONATIONS WELCOME!

Miss Maus glanced up again and saw Polly looking at her. "Is there something I can help you with?" she whispered.

Polly grinned. *There sure is*, she thought.

❊ Chapter 6 ❊

Polly was not an early bird, but on Saturday she was dressed and in the kitchen by 8 a.m. There were lots of books to pack up, and she wanted to get to the library before it got busy. That way, Miss Maus and her father would have a chance to chat.

And maybe fall in love! she thought hopefully.

Polly eyed her dad's cookbooks. There were three whole shelves of them. Where to begin?

Well, the Winklers could definitely live without *101 Ways to Cook Chilli*, she decided, putting it in the carton. *Sprouts, Sprouts, Sprouts! The Ultimate Guide* could go, too. And then there was *Pizza from Around the World* – that was the book with the recipe for tofu pizza.

So long! Farewell! Goodbye! thought Polly, as she pulled book after book off the shelves.

"Sweetie! What are you doing?" Dr Winkler asked. He was standing in the kitchen doorway, still wearing his pyjamas. His hair was sticking up at the back.

"There's a book sale at the library," Polly explained. "I'm collecting books to donate."

"But I still use those cookbooks!" Dr Winkler said.

Polly put her hands on her hips. "Dad, don't be selfish. This is for a really good cause." *Like finding us a mum,* she added to herself. "Besides, if you donate these books, you can get some new ones."

Dr Winkler sighed. "I suppose that's true. But wait – I have to keep that one. It has the lentil loaf recipe!"

Polly sighed and put *Eat Lentils to Keep Fit* back on the shelf. "OK, but you'll drive me to the library, won't you?" she asked her father.

To Polly's dismay, her dad took a long time to get ready. First, he drank coffee. Then, he took a shower. Then, he had the nerve to read the newspaper!

"Come on, Dad! We're going to be late!" Polly complained.

"I don't think those books are going anywhere," Dr Winkler told her. But he finally picked up the car keys. "Say, Polly, that reminds me," he said as they headed out the door. "Did you hear the joke about the maths book that had a problem. . .?"

It was a chilly, foggy morning. As they pulled out of the driveway, Polly couldn't help noticing how spooky the Kreeps' mansion looked, rising out of the mist. And was that a *bat* circling one of the towers? Polly craned her neck to see. But a second later, they turned the corner and the mansion disappeared from view.

When they got to the library, the car park was almost full. Inside the reading room, people milled around, looking at the books for sale. Polly spotted Miss Maus standing by a table piled high with more books.

"Thank you for coming," Miss Maus whispered as Polly and her dad approached with their box. "Would you mind putting your books over there?" She pointed to a long table with a DONATIONS sign on it.

"Happy to," said Dr Winkler, not looking very happy at all.

"Dad," Polly said as he set down the box, "why don't you go and talk to Miss Maus? She's really nice."

"The librarian? Er, OK." Her father looked confused. But he walked over to Miss Maus. "Hi," he said.

"Hello," Miss Maus whispered.

"What's that?" Dr Winkler put a hand to his ear.

"I said 'hello'," Miss Maus told him in a slightly louder whisper.

"Oh, right," said Dr Winkler. There was a long silence. Then he cleared his throat. "So, do you know which building in town has the most storeys?"

"Which one?" Miss Maus whispered.

"The library!" Dr Winkler exclaimed.

Miss Maus blinked.

"Get it?" said Dr Winkler, chuckling. "The library has lots of stories. . ."

Miss Maus didn't even crack a smile. Polly silently groaned.

"Dad," she whispered, "why don't you ask Miss Maus if she has any hobbies."

But her father wasn't listening. Something by the door had caught his attention. Polly turned to see Veronica Kreep enter the library. She was carrying a huge stack of books. Her daughter, Esmerelda, trailed behind her.

Dr Winkler hurried over to her. "Let me help you with that," he said, taking the books from Veronica's arms.

"Thank you, that's very kind," Veronica said. "I had extra copies of all these and I thought, what better place to bring them than the library, where everyone can enjoy them? Did you come to donate books, too?" she asked Dr Winkler.

"Of course!" said Dr Winkler. He set the books on the table with a thud. "Er, after all, it's for a great cause."

Polly's eyes widened as she read the titles of Veronica's books: *Make Your Own Mummy*, *A Guide to Poisonous Plants*,

Understanding Reptiles, *Snake Charming for Dummies*. . .

"Esme, darling," Veronica said to her daughter, "give the librarian your book."

Esme walked over to Miss Maus. She held out a book called *Little Vampire Goes to the Dentist*.

"Thank you," the librarian whispered. But as she reached to take the book, Miss Maus suddenly sneezed: *Achoo! Achoo! Achoo! Achoo!* Four times in a row, each one louder than the last. For such a quiet person, Miss Maus had the noisiest sneezes Polly had ever heard.

"Gracious!" The librarian sniffled. "I don't know what's got into me. Usually cats are the only things that make me sneeze."

Polly leaned over to her father. "Maybe you should get Miss Maus a tissue," she whispered.

But Dr Winkler didn't hear her. He was busy talking to Veronica. "Do you know why no one will kiss Dracula?" Polly heard him say.

Veronica's eyes lit up. "No, why?" she asked.

"Because he has bat breath!" Dr Winkler exclaimed.

Veronica laughed. "You know," she said, lowering her voice, "I've heard the same thing about him."

This is going all wrong! Polly thought. Her dad was supposed to be talking to Miss Maus, not Veronica Kreep. She hoped Veronica would take Esme and leave soon.

But where was Esme? Polly glanced around, but the little girl had disappeared.

Mrow!

Polly looked down and saw a small black cat brushing against the leg of the table. It stared up at Polly with huge green eyes.

Something about that cat is familiar. . . Polly thought.

Before Polly could figure out where she'd seen the cat before, it suddenly leaped on to the table. Miss Maus screamed. Even her scream sounded like a whisper.

"Who let a – *Achoo!* – cat in here?" she whisper-shouted.

"Oh, dear," Veronica said, looking over. "I believe that cat's with me."

"There aren't supposed to be cats in the – *Achoo!* – library!" Miss Maus whispered furiously. "I'm – *Achoo!* – highly allergic to them! *Achoo! Achoo! Achoo!*"

Miss Maus sneezed so hard, she bumped into a table. Books flew everywhere. People turned to see what all the noise was about.

"Somebody please get that cat out of

here!" the librarian squeaked between sneezes. Her nose was bright red, and her eyes were streaming.

Polly tried to grab the kitten, but it slipped through her arms. It dashed through the library, with people shouting and trying to catch it.

At last Polly thought she had it cornered. She crept around a bookshelf, ready to grab it.

But the cat was nowhere in sight. Instead, Polly found Esme.

"Did you see the cat? Where did it go?" Polly asked the little girl. Esme just giggled.

Polly searched all around. But the cat had mysteriously vanished.

By the time Polly returned to the book sale, the librarian had vanished, too. "Where's Miss Maus?" Polly asked her father.

He shrugged. "She went home to take her

allergy medicine," he said. "But if you ask me, she shouldn't be working in a library anyway. She's the noisiest person I've ever met!"

Polly sighed and mentally crossed Miss Maus off her list.

❊ Chapter 7 ❊

"Wow," Mike said on Monday. "Miss Maus really sneezed so hard she knocked over a pile of books?"

Polly nodded. "It was a mess."

The two friends were sitting on the front steps after school, waiting for Petey so they could walk home together.

"So then what happened?" asked Mike.

Polly shrugged. "My dad took home loads of Veronica Kreep's books. He spent all weekend reading *A Tale of Two Cemeteries*."

"Weird," said Mike.

"Weird is right," Polly said. "Those freaky

Kreeps ruin everything! Every time I find a mum for us, they get in the way."

"I don't know," Mike said. "They don't seem so bad to me."

"You don't know the half of it," Polly told him. "Did I tell you that their door knocker is shaped like a dragon? And do you know what Veronica is growing in their flower boxes?"

"Flowers?" Mike guessed.

"Poison ivy!" Polly exclaimed.

"You sure pay a lot of attention to them," Mike remarked.

"Believe me, if your neighbours were as weird as mine, you'd pay attention, too," Polly said. She checked her watch. "I wonder where Petey is? Usually he's not this late getting out of—"

"F-a-t-h-e-a-d!"

"D-i-m-w-i-t!"

The sound of angry voices cut Polly off.

An instant later, Petey charged out of school with a plump blond boy behind him. Petey's face was flushed, and the other boy's hands were balled into fists.

"N-i-m-c-o-n-p-o-o-p!" screamed the boy, spit flying.

"It's nin*com*poop, you nerdbrain!" corrected Petey. "N-i-*n*-c-o-*m*-p-o-o-p." He was so worked up that he didn't even see Polly.

"Wow, he really *is* a good speller," Mike whispered. Polly nodded.

The other boy opened his mouth to reply, when a blue convertible pulled up to the kerb, its horn blaring. A pretty woman sat behind the wheel. She had long eyelashes and wavy blonde hair.

She looks just like a film star, Polly thought.

"Martin!" called the woman. The plump boy whirled around, startled. "Hurry up! You're going to be late for your cello lesson!"

"J-e-r-k!" Martin hissed at Petey. He ran over and jumped into the car. His mum handed him a fizzy drink and a bag from a fast-food restaurant. Then, with a squeal of tyres, they sped off.

Polly and Mike stared after them.

"Wow," said Mike.

"Wow is right!" said Polly. "His mum drives a convertible! And she brings him snacks from Cheez-n-Freeze! How cool is that?"

Petey walked over to them. He was still breathing hard.

"Who was that kid?" Polly asked him.

"Martin Dribbs," Petey said sourly. "He thinks he's smarter than everyone else. He keeps saying he'll beat me in the spelling competition."

Polly stood up and brushed off the seat of her trousers. As casually as she could, she asked, "What's his mother like?"

Petey stared at her. "His mother?! How should I know?"

Mike rolled his eyes. "Uh-oh. Here we go again."

Polly ignored him. "Well, what about his dad?" she asked Petey.

Petey looked at her like she'd grown a second head. "I don't know anything about his dad," he said. "I think his parents are divorced or something. Why do you care?"

"No reason," Polly chirped. She pictured her father sitting next to pretty Ms Dribbs at the spelling competition. And suddenly the day seemed much, much brighter.

❧ Chapter 8 ❧

L et's sit here, Dad," Polly said. She
steered her father to a place on a
bench right next to Ms Dribbs. It was
Wednesday afternoon. Any minute now, the
school spelling competition would start.

The gym was full of kids and parents. But
in Polly's opinion, nobody looked half as
good as Martin's mum. Ms Dribbs was
wearing a cream-coloured jumper, denim
crop trousers and lots of tinkly gold charm
bracelets. Her blonde hair cascaded over
her shoulders in soft waves.

As they took their seats, Dr Winkler
nodded at Ms Dribbs. "Hi," he said.

"Hello," she replied coolly.

Not perfect, Polly thought, *but at least it's a start.*

"Is your child in the spelling competition, too?" Polly's dad asked.

Ms Dribbs nodded. "My son, Martin. He's going to win."

"I'm sure he'll do very well," Dr Winkler said.

"No, he's going to win," Ms Dribbs insisted. "My Martin always comes in first. He's—"

"Yoo-hoo!" a cheery voice broke in. Polly looked up and saw Veronica Kreep and her three kids making their way over to them. Polly felt a ping of dread, like an elastic band snapping in her chest.

"How nice to see you here, Polly!" Veronica said as she took the empty seat next to her. She leaned over to tap Dr Winkler's arm with a long, red fingernail. "Hello to you, too."

"Hi, Veronica!" Dr Winkler replied. "I didn't realize your kids went to school here."

"They don't. But we were thrilled when we heard there was going to be a spelling competition," Veronica said. "We wouldn't have missed it for anything."

Vincent, Damon and Esme all nodded. To Polly's surprise, they really did look excited.

Veronica gazed around the gymnasium as if she'd never seen anything like it. "This is so amazing!" she said. "I've never been to one of these before."

"A spelling competition?" Dr Winkler asked.

"No. A school," Veronica replied.

"Huh?" Polly, Dr Winkler and even Ms Dribbs turned to stare at Veronica.

"But don't your kids go to school?" Polly asked.

"They're home-schooled," Veronica explained. "They always have been *gifted*," she confided in a whisper.

Ms Dribbs pursed her lips disapprovingly. "How do you expect them to get into a decent university?" she asked Veronica.

"Oh, I'm not worried," said Veronica with a wave of her hand. "They get the best tutors. And I make sure they study all the important subjects – maths, reading, astrology. . ."

"Martin will get into any university he wants," Ms Dribbs said. "I'm making sure of that. He plays the cello, he's number one in his fencing league and he's practically fluent in Finnish."

"It's pretty early to be thinking about university. After all, they're only in primary school," Dr Winkler remarked.

"You can never start too soon." Ms Dribbs sniffed.

A whistle blew, and Mr Webster, Polly's PE teacher, stepped into the centre of the gymnasium. He tapped the microphone and welcomed everybody. The spelling competition was about to begin.

Polly sneaked one last glance at the Kreeps. They were all sitting on the edges of their seats.

They sure must like spelling, she thought.

An hour later, the spelling competition was going into its third round. Both Petey and Martin were still in the running, along with six other kids.

Every time Petey spelled a word, Polly held her breath. It didn't matter to Polly if he lost, but she knew it mattered to Petey. And for his sake, she wanted him to win.

It was Martin's turn next. "The word is 'nincompoop'," Mr Webster said.

A few people laughed, but Polly gasped. Petey had *given* Martin the correct spelling of the word just a few days before. Would Martin remember it now?

"Nincompoop," he began. "N-i—"

Martin hesitated. He chewed his lip, thinking.

Just then, Polly heard a quiet jingle. She looked around. The sound was coming from Ms Dribbs' charm bracelet. Ms Dribbs was running a finger up and down her nose, as if she were scratching it.

And, Polly suddenly realized, Martin was watching her.

He cleared his throat and said, "n-i-**n**-c-o—"

Once again he hesitated. And once again Polly heard that soft jingling. She looked over and saw Ms Dribbs tapping a finger to her mouth.

Martin said, "**m**-p-o-o-p. Nincompoop."

"Correct," said Mr Webster.

I don't believe it! thought Polly. *Ms Dribbs is sending Martin signals!* Touching her nose meant *n*, and tapping her mouth meant *m*!

Polly wanted to jump up and tell the whole gymnasium that Martin and his mother were cheating. But. . .

But what if I'm wrong? she thought.

Suddenly Polly felt uncertain. After all, people were always telling her that she had a big imagination.

Polly glanced over at her father. He was smiling. He certainly didn't look like he had noticed anything.

If I call Martin's mum a cheater, she'll never want to go out with my dad, Polly thought. She decided to keep quiet – at least until she was sure.

After another round, Petey and Martin

were the only contestants left. Petey had just finished spelling 'catastrophe', when Esme suddenly tugged on her mother's sleeve.

"Mummy!" she whispered. "I think I lost Bubbles!"

Veronica sighed. "Oh, darling. You didn't bring Bubbles *here*, did you?"

Esme's eyes filled with tears. "I couldn't leave her at home," she cried. "She gets lonely without me."

She looked so sad, Polly's heart went out to her. "Is Bubbles your kitty?" she asked.

Esme sniffled and shook her head. "No. Bubbles is my—"

"*Shhhh!*" Ms Dribbs was holding a finger to her lips and glaring at them. "Be quiet. It's Martin's turn!"

"The word is 'cauliflower'," Mr Webster told Martin.

"Cauliflower," said Martin. "C-a-u-l—"

He hesitated, then stole a glance at his mother.

Polly was watching Ms Dribbs, too. The woman started to reach a finger towards her face.

I was right! Polly thought. *She is cheating!*

But before she could say anything, Ms Dribbs suddenly leaped up from her seat. "*Eeeeeee!*" she shrieked.

Martin smiled and turned back to Mr Webster. "E!" he said confidently. "C-a-u-l-e-f-l-o-w-e-r. Cauliflower!"

Mr Webster pressed a buzzer. "Sorry, Martin," he said. "That's incorrect."

"But . . . but. . ." Martin began to protest. He looked over at his mother. But she hadn't even noticed he'd got the word wrong. She was still hopping around, and now Polly saw why – a giant tarantula was crawling up her leg.

"Bubbles!" Esme exclaimed, scooping the spider up.

Ms Dribbs snatched up her handbag and went running for the door.

"Ha!" Polly whispered. "Serves you right, you cheater!"

Meanwhile, Petey was spelling the word: "C-a-u-l-i-f-l-o-w-e-r."

"That's correct," said Mr Webster, smiling. "Congratulations, Peter Winkler! You are now Champion Speller of Endsville Primary School!"

Petey's face split into a huge grin. The audience clapped as Mr Webster handed him a trophy. Polly whistled through her front teeth, and Joy, who was sitting in the front row with her friends, started a cheer.

The only people who weren't cheering were the Kreeps. As the noise started to die down, Polly overheard Vincent say, "That's it? What kind of spelling competition was that?"

"What a waste of time!" Damon snapped.

Even Esme looked disappointed. "What happened, Mummy? Why weren't there any spells?"

Spells?! Polly's ears perked up. Just what did the Kreeps think a spelling competition was?

"I don't know, darling," Veronica told Esme. Veronica looked back at Petey, who was getting his picture taken with his trophy. And for the first time since Polly had met her, she looked completely bewildered.

✢ Chapter 9 ✢

Polly was truly happy for her brother. But as they returned home, her spirits were low. She had to admit Mission Mum was a total flop.

And to make things worse, her project on Moldova was due in just two days. She'd been so busy trying to find her family a mum, she hadn't written a single word.

Polly slumped on her front steps, her chin in her hands. *No mum. No project,* she thought. *Zero plus zero equals zero.* She felt as if her own personal rain cloud was hanging over her head.

Across the street, she noticed, there really *was* a rain cloud hanging over the Kreeps' mansion. Veronica was in the front garden, throwing scraps of meat to the Venus flytraps. When she saw Polly, she waved.

"Petey did a wonderful job today," Veronica said.

"Yeah," Polly replied sadly. "We're all proud of him."

Veronica was silent for a moment. Then she crossed the street and came over to Polly. "Why the sad face?" she asked.

Polly sighed. "My family is weird," she told Veronica.

"Says who?" Veronica asked.

"This girl at school. And other people, too, probably." Polly wasn't sure why she was telling this to Veronica. But the woman didn't seem to mind. She was listening attentively.

Veronica sat down next to her. "So what if they're weird?" she asked Polly.

Polly shrugged. "It's embarrassing."

Veronica smoothed her skirt thoughtfully. "You love your family, though, right?" she asked.

"Yeah." Polly nodded.

"And they love you, I'm sure."

Polly nodded again.

"Well, that's the most important thing," said Veronica. "That's sort of what having a family is about: loving them even when they're weird."

Polly thought about that. Maybe Veronica had a point. Maybe her family was fine just the way it was.

"But that's not my only problem," Polly said. "I have to do this project, but I can't find any books, and I can't use the Internet. I've had two whole weeks to do it, and I haven't done a thing. And it's due the day after tomorrow!" Polly put her head in her hands. The more she thought about it, the worse it seemed.

"What's the project on?" Veronica asked.

"Moldova," Polly told her. "It's a country, not a cheese."

"Moldova. Hmm," said Veronica. "That is a tough one. But I think I have just the thing to help you."

Polly shook her head. "Nothing can help me now, unless. . ." Polly's voice trailed off. Veronica was smiling at her mysteriously. In her pointy boots and floppy black hat, she looked more like a witch than ever.

Maybe she really is a witch, Polly thought. *And if she's a witch, that means she can do magic!* She pictured Veronica waving a wand and making her project appear.

"Do you have your wa – er, thing here?" Polly asked eagerly.

Veronica laughed. "No, it's at home, of course," she said.

"Well, what are we waiting for?" Polly hopped up from the porch and called into her house, "Dad, I'm going over to the Kreeps' house. I'll be back soon!" She turned to Veronica and said, "Let's go!"

Polly and Veronica crossed the street and walked up the rickety front steps. Polly paused at the sight of the dragon-shaped door knocker. Then she shook her head and followed Veronica inside.

The inside of the Kreeps' house turned out to be even stranger than the outside. In the front hallway, coats and capes were piled on two stone gargoyles. A stuffed crocodile sat in the corner, propping up a heap of umbrellas.

I did see a crocodile the day they moved in! she thought. She couldn't wait to tell Mike.

"Don't mind the mess. We're still unpacking," Veronica said, leading her through another room. She stepped around a box filled with crumpled newspapers, and Polly caught a glimpse of a crystal ball nestled inside. Around the room, portraits of pale, ghostly-looking people leaned against the walls, waiting to be hung. And over by the window Polly spied a witch's cauldron with a potted palm growing out of it.

Polly wondered what kind of magic Veronica would do to make her project appear. Would she say a spell? Or make some kind of potion? Or maybe she had a magic pen that could write on its own!

They walked down the hall and turned into a large room. Polly looked around. There was nothing but rows and rows of books, from the floor all the way to the ceiling.

Veronica went to a bookshelf so tall that she had to use a ladder. She pulled three books from the top shelf and climbed down.

"Here you are," she said, handing them to Polly. "They're all about Moldova."

Polly blinked. "Books? You mean . . . I have to *read* them?"

"How else did you think your project would get done? Magic?" Veronica's green eyes twinkled. "Be sure to read the marked pages," she added.

Polly looked down, and her mouth fell open in surprise. The books were bristling with bookmarks. They hadn't been there a second before. She was sure of it!

She turned to Veronica for an explanation, but Veronica just smiled mysteriously and ushered Polly out.

At the door, Polly thought of something. "Why do you have so many books on Moldova, anyway?" she asked.

"I used to live near there," Veronica told her.

Polly frowned. "You mean Kansas?"

"No," Veronica said. "Transylvania." And with a wink, she closed the door.

❧ Chapter 10 ❧

The following week, Polly was waiting for her dad when he got home from work.

"Guess what," she said as he walked through the door. "I got an A!" She held up her project on Moldova and showed him the gold star at the top.

"'*Moldova: Nothing Mouldy About It,*'" he said, reading the title. "That's fantastic, honey. I'm going to have to read this whole thing. It sounds like I can learn a lot."

"My teacher said it was one of the best projects," Polly told her dad. She smiled to herself, thinking of Denise's face when she'd heard that. When Denise got her project back, she'd quickly folded it and put it in her desk, but not before Polly had seen the big letter *C* written on it. *I guess Denise's mum didn't know so much about France after all,* Polly thought.

She took her project back from her dad. "I'm going to take it to show Veronica," she told him. "She helped me a lot."

Her dad got a funny look on his face. "About Veronica—" he said.

Before he could finish, the doorbell rang. Polly answered it. Veronica was standing on their doorstep. Today she had on a long, midnight blue dress and earrings made of peacock feathers.

"I was just coming to see you!" Polly exclaimed. "I got an A on my project."

"Wonderful!" Veronica said, giving her a hug. "I knew you would."

82

"Hello, Veronica!" Dr Winkler said, coming into the front hallway.

"Hi Wally," she replied. "Ready to go?"

Polly looked back and forth between them. "Go where?" she asked.

"There's a reading at the library," her dad explained. "The author of *A Tale of Two Cemeteries* will be there."

"He's my favourite writer," Veronica gushed. "His books are *so* inspiring."

"Joy will be here," Dr Winkler told Polly. "And I'll have my mobile phone if anything comes up." He turned to Veronica. "Shall we?"

Veronica smiled. "Ready when you are."

"I sure hope that noisy librarian isn't there this time," Polly heard her dad say as they headed towards the car.

My dad and Veronica – friends?! she thought. *Too weird!* As far as Polly could tell, they didn't have anything in common.

But if her dad wanted to have a weird friend, that was OK with her. After all, Veronica was awfully nice.

And besides, Polly thought as she watched them drive away, *what's the worst that can happen?*

✤ Epilogue ✤

Three months later. . .

The sun had set, and the last dregs of light were fading from the sky over Pleasant Street. From her living room window, Polly could see Vincent, Damon and Esmerelda Kreep out on their front lawn. They were playing a game of catch.

The Kreeps seemed to be having a great time. They were laughing and yelling to one another. *They almost seem like a normal family*, Polly thought. *Except. . .*

Polly leaned closer to the glass.

There was something strange about that ball.

Just then, Vincent threw the ball, sending it high up in the sky. As it spun through the air, Polly caught a glimpse of a face and a patch of tangled hair. Her jaw dropped.

It wasn't a ball at all. It was a shrunken head!

"Polly!"

Polly jumped and spun around. Her dad was standing in the doorway.

"I've been looking all over for you, honey," he said. "What are you doing in here with the lights off?" He switched on a lamp and warm light filled the room.

Polly noticed Joy and Petey were standing behind him. "What's up?" she asked.

"I wanted to talk with you three kids together," their father said.

"OK." Polly raised her eyebrows at Joy

and Petey to say *what's going on?* They both shrugged.

Polly, her brother and her sister sat down. "Polly, it's r-u-d-e to put your feet on the coffee table, remember?" Petey said smugly.

Polly sighed and lowered her feet to the floor. Ever since she'd taught Petey about manners, he'd gone nuts for them. She almost missed the old days when he used to chew with his mouth full and pick his nose.

As soon as everyone was settled, Dr Winkler cleared his throat. Then he cleared it again. "You know I've been out a lot lately," he began.

"With Veronica," Petey said helpfully.

"Yes, with Veronica." Their father paused and cleared his throat again. He looked a little worried.

"We don't mind," Polly said quickly.

Whenever her dad and Veronica went out, Polly and her siblings got to order pizza. The Winklers' smoke alarm hadn't gone off for weeks, and for that, Polly was grateful.

"I think it's great that she's teaching you about so many fun hobbies," Joy chimed in. "Like fire walking and growing flesh-eating plants."

"Thanks, Joy," Dr Winkler said. "But there's more to it than just hobbies. You see, Veronica has a certain magic. . ."

Magic? Polly thought, her eyes growing wide. Did her dad know that Veronica was a witch? Maybe that's why he looked so worried. He was afraid she might cast an evil spell!

I should tell him he has nothing to worry about, Polly thought. She was pretty sure that even if Veronica was a witch, she was a good one.

"Dad, don't worry," Polly said. "I think

that Veronica is a really nice wi – er, person."

Her dad smiled with relief. "I'm so glad to hear you say that, Polly. Because what I've been trying to say is, Veronica and I are getting married!"

"*Married?!*" Polly's mouth fell open. Silence filled the room as the three kids stared at their dad.

"Wow," Joy said finally, giving their dad a hug. "That's awesome!"

"W-o-w," Petey echoed.

"W—" Polly tried to say. But the word stuck in her throat.

She glanced out the window. Across the street, she could see Vincent, Damon and Esme still playing their game of catch-the-head.

I don't believe it, Polly thought. *The creepy Kreeps are going to be my family!*

Polly's adventures with
the Kreeps continue in

Meet
the
Kreeps

The New Step-Mummy

Polly Winkler sat at the kitchen table, trying to eat her breakfast. It was a bright summer morning. Out the window, she could see sprinklers watering her neighbour's front lawn and birds fluttering around the trees. *Outside, it seems like a normal day*, Polly thought. But inside the Winklers' house, things were anything *but* normal.

"No, no, no!" her father, Wally Winkler, exclaimed into the phone, a cup of coffee sloshing in one hand. "We ordered steak for two dozen – *steak*, not *snake*! Where on earth did you get that idea?"

Polly scooped a spoonful of cornflakes into her mouth and grimly chewed. It was hard to enjoy her breakfast amid all the commotion. Her sister, Joy, was also shouting. Joy was a cheerleader, and her voice really carried.

"Did you call the florist, Dad?" she cried. "What about the balloons? You can't have a wedding without balloons!"

Finally, Polly put down her spoon. *It's official*, she thought. *My family has gone completely bonkers*. And Polly was sure that her "famous imagination" wasn't to blame this time.

In just two days, Dr Winkler was getting married, and it seemed to Polly like her family had gone wedding crazy. The only person who wasn't in a frenzy was Polly's brother, Petey. He was calmly sitting at the breakfast table, looking at the dictionary.

Polly nudged him with her toe. "It's rude to read at the table, Petey," she reminded him.

Petey looked up, annoyed. "Well, it's rude

to touch people with your feet," he said. "Besides, I'm not reading. I'm memorizing."

"The *dictionary*?" asked Polly.

"It's the best place to find spelling words," he replied. Petey was the Endsville Primary spelling champion, a fact that he often liked to bring up.

"But it's summertime," Polly pointed out. "Nobody memorizes stuff in the summer."

"I don't want to lose my competitive edge," Petey said with a shrug. He went back to studying.

Polly sighed. *Petey hasn't gone wedding crazy*, she thought. *He's just plain old crazy.*

Just then, a knock came at their back door. Polly got up to answer it. Veronica Kreep, Polly's soon-to-be stepmother, was standing there, along with her three children – Vincent, Damon, and Esmerelda.

"Veronica!" Dr Winkler cried when he saw

her. He hung up the phone and hurried over to kiss her pale cheek.

"I tried to call before we came," Veronica said apologetically. "But the line has been busy all morning."

"I've been on the phone making sure everything is set for the wedding," Dr Winkler explained. "You wouldn't believe how the caterer mixed up our order!"

"How odd," said Veronica, frowning. "I spoke with them just yesterday, and everything seemed fine."

"Well, don't worry," Dr Winkler said, squeezing her hand. "I got it all straightened out." Watching them, Polly wondered, not for the first time, how her father and Veronica had ever fallen in love. Veronica was not at all like Polly's goofy, dentist dad. In fact she wasn't like anyone Polly had ever met. Instead of jeans and trainers, Veronica wore long, black dresses and pointy boots.

Instead of flowers, she grew carnivorous plants. And when she cleaned, Veronica didn't dust away the spiderwebs – she dusted *around* them.

Veronica's kids were as strange as she was. Vincent, the oldest, was tall and pale. He always wore a black hooded sweatshirt, and he almost never smiled. Damon, his younger brother, smiled all the time. But it was a crafty smile, like he was up to something. Damon's hair stuck straight up on his head, and he often wore a lab coat and safety goggles. Esmerelda, the youngest, had a thin, white face, pigtails, and huge, green eyes. Her favourite pet was a tarantula named Bubbles. Polly couldn't imagine having them as her brothers and sister any more than she could imagine having Veronica as a mother.

The problem was, the rest of her family didn't seem to think there was anything weird about the Kreeps. When Polly pointed out that the Kreeps' car looked like a hearse, her dad said, "Don't be silly, Polly." When she mentioned that she'd seen bats flying around the Kreeps' house, her sister told her she was imagining things. Polly was known for having a vivid imagination. But she didn't think she was imagining that there was something truly strange about the Kreeps.

"What are you all doing out so early?" Dr Winkler asked Veronica now.

"We're on our way back from the airport," she replied. "We were picking up Uncle Vlad."

"Uncle Vlad?" Dr Winkler scratched his head. "I don't remember you mentioning him."

"Of course I did, darling," Veronica said. "He's on the Transylvanian side of the family. He took an overnight flight."

"Well, why don't you bring him in?" asked Dr Winkler. "I'd love to meet him."

"He's asleep in the car," Veronica said with a little frown. "And I'd rather not wake him up. He's not much of a morning person."

"You can say that again," Vincent remarked with a snort.

"Anyway," said Veronica, "I just wanted to stop by and let the girls know that the bridesmaid dresses are ready. They can come over and try them on this afternoon."

"Awesome!" cried Joy, throwing her arms around Veronica. "I'm so excited for the wedding!"

"Er, I'm glad, dear," Veronica gasped. Her eyes bugged a little from Joy's tight squeeze.

Dr Winkler checked his watch. "I'd better get going," he said. "I've got a lot to do today."

"We have to be going, too," Veronica said. "We'll see you girls this afternoon."

The Kreeps filed out. But at the door, Veronica turned. "You know," she said, "maybe I should check in with the caterer again. Just to make sure they have our order right."

"Good idea," said Dr Winkler, who was already on the phone. He waved goodbye.

"After all," Veronica said to no one in particular, "a party just isn't a party without roasted rattlesnake."

She gave Polly a wink, then turned and headed out the door.

Polly stared after her. *Rattlesnake?* she thought. *This wedding is getting crazier by the minute!*

If you like
creepy stories,
you'll love

Turn the page for more
chills and thrills. . .

THE ORIGINAL SERIES FROM THE MASTER OF FRIGHT!

Goosebumps®

NIGHT of the LIVING DUMMY

R.L. STINE

NOW with BONUS FEATURES!

The original bone-chilling series
is back — now featuring
Behind-the-Screams bonus content!

Fright-master R.L. Stine is back with an all-new, all-terrifying series! Enter HorrorLand — if you dare...